About the Author

The author lives in the Scottish Highlands with his wife Linda and their Collie called Holly, he works from home as paramedic for the Scottish Ambulance Service in the village of Lochcarron.

He is a member of the Lochcarron writing group and enjoys the Scottish wildlife, landscapes and photography.

Dedication

Dedicated to the Howard Doris Centre Lochcarron, which gave me the inspiration for this book and my good friend Mary Henery who patiently helped me towards the final draft.

To my brother Clive who sadly died on 11th May 2016, taken too early. He loved Lochcarron and the Highlands of Scotland, but sadly didn't live to see this book published.

Stanley Jackson

THE LOCHCARRON SPACE PROGRAMME

CATS IN SPACE

AUSTIN MACAULEY
PUBLISHERS LTD.

A CIP catalogue record for this title is available from the British Library.

ISBN 9781786126689 (Paperback)
ISBN 9781786126696 (Hardback)
ISBN 9781786126702 (E-Book)

www.austinmacauley.com

First Published (2016)
Austin Macauley Publishers Ltd.
25 Canada Square
Canary Wharf
London
E14 5LQ

Chapter 1

The Planning

Howard and Doris lived at The Howard Doris Community Care Centre in Lochcarron, a small village in the Highlands of Scotland. They were friends with all the humans who lived, worked or visited there. Howard was a big tom who liked to be stroked and made a fuss of while Doris was a timid tabby who needed to get to know you before you became her friend. As insider cats they spent their days wandering around all the rooms, listening to stories the residents told of what they had gotten up to as children and the adventures they had with their family and friends. Now the cats talked constantly and dreamed of things they might do.

One night when all was quiet, Howard and Doris sat in the foyer looking out of the window at a bright white disc in the sky. The cats were lucky because in the foyer was a selection of library books left for the humans to borrow and return when the library was closed. This gave them the chance to look at the books and come up with ideas for their big adventure.

A few nights later they came across two books, one on astronomy and another on space travel. The first book was hard to understand but they worked out that the bright white disc they had seen was the moon and the book on space travel told them how rockets were built. They also remembered seeing programs on television and were big fans of Wallace and Gromit's "A Grand Day Out" where they had a trip to the moon, and at that moment the decision was made to build a space ship and become the pioneers of the Lochcarron Space Programme, "Cats in Space." Howard and Doris set to work immediately, as they had many nights of hard work ahead of them, drawing up a list of things they needed. The village was small but they were sure that around the village they could find all that was needed and laughed at the thought of becoming cat burglars to get everything they required.

Next day Howard and Doris quietly got on with their daily lives, meeting humans and getting stroked by the staff and residents, who thought they were just two cats and would be very surprised if they knew what they were planning. It wasn't easy hiding their excitement from their human friends, who might interfere with their adventure. What they needed to do was sleep during the day and work longer and harder on the space programme at night. They also decided that only one would be an active participant in the daily activities while the other would sleep and then swap roles and catnap, hoping the humans would be too busy to notice as they cared for the elderly.

Howard was in one of the humans' rooms watching a programme on television showing schools competing in a national competition, where they had to design and build a rocket and then fire it up into the sky, with a prize for the longest and highest flights. Howard tried to memorize the building process and what was needed to make a space rocket that flew. Unfortunately he had had a big dinner and fell asleep, purring like a train. When he eventually woke

6

up the programme had finished, so he had a big stretch and went to find Doris and tell her what he could remember about the space rockets, building them and getting them to fly, but also that he had missed most of it as he had fallen asleep.

Chapter 2

Outside Helpers

Each evening as the daily activities of the humans slowed down. Staff went home, visitors said "Cheerio," and everyone went to bed. This lull allowed Howard and Doris to get back to their planning and deciding on what was going to be needed. They realised they needed some help, because they had never been out and therefore did not know what was beyond the big building they lived in. An outsider was needed, and someone they had seen out and about in the dark hours. The two who came to mind were Pierre, the local pine marten and Olivia, the short eared owl, who often came to the window at night.

When everyone had gone to their rooms and the night staff were busying themselves with their work, Howard and Doris could settle down in the foyer with their books and continue planning the Lochcarron Space Programme. Leafing through books on flying, engines, astronomy and maps of the local area, it did not take them long to realise that they were only cats and it would be impossible for a cat to build an engine from scratch, so they would have to find one ready-made. Tonight they would just keep an eye open for Pierre and Olivia and use their knowledge of the outside world and perhaps the task would become less daunting.

Not speaking, but both thinking of the adventure that lay ahead of them, they watched the moon which seemed an awfully long way away and had the bad habit of disappearing behind the clouds. That worried them a bit. All of a sudden Pierre appeared, looking his usual regal self. He always came to see them and they knew he would help if he could. Pierre came right up to the doors, sat down and sniffed the calm night air. They looked through the glass at each other; then suddenly Doris started talking non-stop. She told Pierre everything about their plans of going into space and why they needed help. Howard and Pierre looked at her. She gave them a glance as if to say, "What?"

Howard grinned, "Doris, you are so excited, I have never seen you like this before."

"We've never planned on going into space before," she replied.

Pierre was speechless; he could not believe what his insider friend Doris had just told him. "Howard, is Doris being serious?"

"Yes, Pierre that is what we are planning to do, but we really need the help of you and Olivia, our outsider friends."

"Of course we will help, but we know nothing of rockets or going into space."

Pierre set off on his nightly foray and promised to find Olivia as she flew back to her roost in Slumbay, and they would come back together. With that, he slunk off into the darkness, leaving Howard and Doris alone with their thoughts.

Howard and Doris resumed their studies. Howard looked at a map of the area and Doris went on to the

9

internet and tapped in 'space rockets', 'space travel' and millions of sites came up for them to search through. Which would be the best to start with? She decided to click on the first one on the list, this showed a rocket taking off with a loud roar and she called Howard over as it scared her. They sat transfixed as the rocket left the earth and screamed through the air and both their thoughts were the same. Could these two little cats, with the help of their two outsider friends, become cats in space?

Pierre went off towards Slumbay without looking for food, he was so intent on finding Olivia and bringing her back to the centre, so that their adventurous cat friends could tell her about their big plans for going into space. It was hard to imagine these two little cats, whom he had known for some time, had decided to venture outside for the first time and come up with an idea so outrageous as to go into space. He had to find Olivia. He strode on hoping to catch a glimpse of her in the moonlight but an eerie fog drifted in and around the bay. Walking through some bushes a voice called out from above.

"Hi, Pierre." He glanced up and there she sat on an overhanging branch.

"Hello, Olivia, I've been looking for you."

"You looked like you had a purpose to your stride, Pierre, I've been watching you for a while."

Pierre shuddered, thinking how glad he was that owls did not eat pine martens. Pierre explained that Howard and Doris had asked him to find her because they had a big plan, he did not say what it was in case Olivia fell out of the tree in shock.

All he said was, "Will you come back with me and the cats will tell you all about it."

Olivia was intrigued and agreed to go back with Pierre and find out what this big plan was. As the pair made their way back to the care centre they commented on what humans might think if they saw a pine marten and a short eared owl making their way through Lochcarron together. Some insiders' house lights were still on, although it was still dark and during their nightly outings Pierre and Olivia had noticed that not all the insiders had the same routine. Some slept during the day, some had jobs that meant starting really early, some worked from home. One vehicle used to move around the village to different houses and appeared to be owned by five different humans, but the fifth was confusing as he had not been in Lochcarron very long and did not seem to have the vehicle as often as the other five. This vehicle must have been special, because Pierre and Olivia had seen it with blue flashing lights and other vehicles tried to get out of its way.

Pierre and Olivia made it back to the centre, where both Howard and Doris were busy with books and the computer. They did not see Pierre and Olivia coming across the car park, and Howard jumped when he saw something cast a shadow across his book, but it was just their outsider friends and he called Doris from the computer to come and see them. Doris jumped down and went to the foyer window where Pierre, Olivia and Howard were. The window was slightly open so they could talk quietly.

"Pierre has told me that you cats had a big plan and needed some help," said Olivia, "So here I am to find out all about it."

Howard looked at Doris and smiled, letting Doris explain all about how they had been looking for a big adventure after listening to all the stories from the residents. After much consideration they had decided to attempt to get to the moon and be cats in space. Stunned, poor Olivia lost her balance on the window sill and tumbled backwards, but a few quick wing flaps and she managed to land the right way up on the ground, rather shaken up.

Pierre laughed and said, "That's why I did not tell you when you were perched up in the tree."

"I am not too sure how I can help," said Olivia, "But if you tell me what you need from me I will try, although I do believe you are both slightly mad. I can fly, but it would be impossible for me to fly you to the moon, if it is as far away as it looks, so I hope that was not your idea?"

The adventurous cats both said, "No," and purred for a while.

Eventually Howard explained they hoped to build a rocket and launch it from the top of the Bealach Na Ba on a night when there was a full moon and no cloud.

Pierre said, "That is a bit specific."

To which Howard replied, "I know but Doris got scared when the moon disappeared behind the clouds the other night, I don't want a scaredy cat on board on our way to fulfil our destiny or whatever happens after the launch."

Pierre chuckled, which upset Doris. She was thinking of calling it off. She did not like Pierre laughing at her; it was all right for him, he was an outsider and had done adventurous and brave things before; climb hills and trees, cross busy roads. All Howard and Doris had ever done was eat and sleep and be made a fuss of.

With that, Pierre and Olivia said, "We have to go now as the human outsiders will be up soon. We definitely do not want to meet up with them, but we will come back tonight for more instructions."

Howard and Doris remained in the foyer thinking their own thoughts on what Pierre and Olivia could do for them, until the smell of bacon & eggs frying sent Howard off in search of a kind resident who would sneak him a treat.

Chapter 3

Cat Life and Adventure

Doris strolled off to the warmth of a resident's room, where she used to curl up on the foot of the bed and chase mice in her dreams, but now she had real adventure on her mind, her dreams were more exciting and involved thoughts of flying rockets into space. Doris dozed and Howard welcomed residents as they came through for breakfast. In exchange for allowing himself to be stroked, he hoped for a breakfast treat. After a while the residents were seated and serving began. The smells were more tempting than his cat food and soon old Alistair tapped his shoe to signal Howard over. Howard made his way to where Alistair was sitting, casually zigzagging in and out of the table and chair legs, not wanting to make it obvious that he had food on his mind. When Howard arrived at Alistair's table, there beside his foot was a piece of lovely bacon, his wish had come true. Howard ate his treat and wandered off to doze by the library books. Stretching out like a draught excluder, he rolled on to his back. Comfortable now with warm bacon in his tummy, he dozed off. As he started to dream he felt a sharp tap on his cream and black nose and sat up quickly, very annoyed that his sleep had been interrupted. It was

Doris, her sleep had been disturbed too by staff making the bed, so she had come to find Howard. He gave her one of those angry looks and cursed her cattily, but Doris was so sweet he was not angry for very long, and she sat by him in the foyer and chatted about what kind of help Pierre and Olivia could give them.

As the day went on they took it in turns to sleep as agreed and would sometimes stop to pass bits of information about things that should go on the list for Pierre and Olivia. They needed to know if there was access to engines, fuel, wood, electrical wiring, seats, oxygen, drills; all sorts of things which only the outsiders could help them with, as they were insiders. The daylight began to fade and the humans went home and were replaced by the night staff. The cats sat in the foyer listening to the lights clicking off one by one. The centre was almost in darkness. Howard and Doris sat by the foyer window looking out at the moonless night sky, where lots of stars twinkled in the blackness. It was an eerie blackness which Doris did not like. As they sat waiting for Pierre and Olivia to come, they anxiously hoped their two friends had not thought them complete idiots and were just humouring them. These unpleasant and worrying thoughts were soon banished when Pierre and Olivia came across the car park. Both looked happy and were having such a good conversation that Pierre almost walked into a post, Olivia warned him just in time.

After a few minutes of idle chatter about what the day and weather had been like. Olivia butted in and asked how she and Pierre would be able to help this pair of adventurous cats in the Lochcarron Space Programme. Howard explained that he and Doris did not go out into the big world outside the Howard Doris Centre, and they had no idea if Lochcarron had all the things they would need to build a rocket and get it into space. They needed Pierre and Olivia to check the list which Doris gave them for things that could be found around the area, things such as old oil drums, large pipes etc. that might be of use to them.

Pierre and Olivia said they would take a look when doing their rounds tonight.

Pierre said he would have to find some food first, as he was so hungry you could hear his tummy rumbling.

With that, Pierre ran through the car park, across the main road, back the way he had come, around the side of the Blythswood charity shop and into the woods. Olivia flew quietly over the car park, skimming the roof of the Ferguson Medical Centre and off towards Slumbay.

As their two friends went off into the night, Howard and Doris realised their big adventure might take a little bit longer than they had hoped.

But Doris said, "It does not matter that much, Howard. We haven't actually done anything exciting before, but we are planning something now."

Howard had to agree, "You are right as always, Doris, we can still carry on with our plans, and we still have an awful lot to do."

The cats settled down to do their planning and occasionally their ears twitched when they heard staff talking or residents coughing. Otherwise, it was a peaceful place to be a cat. Tonight seemed different though, it was as if the staff knew something was being planned, and they kept passing through the foyer. Howard and Doris did not understand why, and went to find out what was happening. They wandered around big corridors that joined all the residents' rooms until they found a room with lots of staff fussing around. Sarah, their old friend who was lying in bed, sounded confused and the manageress kept cuddling her and telling her she would be okay as the doctor was coming.

Howard and Doris loved Sarah and decided to put their plans on hold and just sit in the doorway and wait for the doctor to arrive. It did not seem very long at all until the doctor, a nice, caring man, arrived and they moved out of the way to let him through. He examined Sarah and said she had some kind of infection, but they could treat her at the centre because it was better for people to stay at home if they could. The doctor left some medication and a glass bottle for some reason and told staff he would be back in the morning, patting the cats' heads as he went. The adventurous cats sat for a while as the staff busied themselves with Sarah. Eventually she dropped off to sleep and the staff carried on with their nightly duties. A pleasant young human said she would sit with Sarah for a while, so Howard and Doris went over to the bed, Doris jumped up and snuggled down by Sarah's feet, while Howard rubbed himself against the legs of the young human and got his ears stroked in return. Howard purred, but suddenly remembered he had plans to get ready and dashed out of the room back to the foyer, making the young human jump. Howard sat alone, as Doris had decided to sleep, but he did not mind as she was keeping Sarah company. He liked being on his own now and again, it gave him time to think and remember stories he had heard from the residents. Not all the stories had been good. He had heard a lot about something called the war, where millions of humans had been killed, all friends or family to somebody. He did not understand all of it, but for some reason he felt sad.

Chapter 4

Is it the End?

Peeking out occasionally from behind the books in the foyer, Howard saw Pierre and Olivia making their way towards him, between the houses as they had before. They must have arranged to meet up, as they had gone in opposite directions and Pierre had only food on his mind. He looked like he had had a very good meal by the size of his tummy and he waddled rather than walked now. Howard decided not to say anything as he did not want to upset his friend.

His friends approached the little window and said, "Hello" and asked where Doris was.

Howard explained that they had been interrupted tonight and Doris had decided to sleep at the foot of the resident's bed to comfort her.

His outsider friends did not sound happy about this. As they had been out trying to help their insider friends, yet one of them was asleep. Howard explained that part of their plan was to act normally so nobody was suspicious, Doris sleeping was actually helping them.

Pierre mumbled something but they left it at that.

Pierre then said they had been all around the village and saw lots of things that could be used. He had found engines in old cars, piping, cable, wood and lots more.

Olivia said she had flown around Slumbay and over to Kishorn and found lots too, but they had the same thought: it was too big for an owl and a pine marten to carry, so there was no way of getting all of the material for a space rocket back to the cats and even if they could, who would build it?

Howard was a little upset. Everything seemed so much harder than they had first thought when they came up with the idea.

Pierre and Olivia said goodnight, but would be back tomorrow.

Maybe, just maybe, Howard and Doris would come up with a solution by then.

Howard sat quietly, just thinking everyday cat thoughts now that the Lochcarron Space Programme was apparently falling down around his ears. He could hear Doris trotting up the corridor, full of life after her sleep, and knew he hadn't the heart to tell his best friend their adventure could be over before it began, so he pretended to be asleep. Doris ambled up beside him, purring, but she realised he was asleep and mumbled something which Howard did not quite hear. This did not please him because he was the one who had been up all night waiting for their friends to return and to listen to the bad news. Doris wanted to ask Howard if Pierre and Olivia had called round before they went home. She needed to know how much information their friends had gathered and discuss what to do next, but Howard was asleep. Most of all she wanted to say sorry for sleeping so long and not helping with any more planning, and not being around if Pierre and Olivia had returned. She decided to let her friend sleep since he was obviously tired, so she quietly made her way back to Sarah's bedroom and jumped on to the bed. Sarah shuffled a bit and groaned but did not wake up, so Doris settled down and went back to sleep.

A new day dawned and people started moving around, getting ready for breakfast. Howard was fast asleep and purring like a steam train until he was rudely awoken by a loud door bell. It was the doctor, coming back to see the lovely Sarah and a member of staff let him in. Howard followed behind the doctor to the room and saw Doris fast asleep on the bed.

Howard thought for a minute, are our plans for an adventure falling apart already? No, it will happen. We only need a plan B, something far less daunting than plan A. I will start thinking right away.

With that thought he trotted back to the foyer, but made a detour to the dining room, hoping for a little bacon treat. Howard poked his head around the door to see who was about. There was a human putting food on plates and another taking them to the ladies and gentlemen, otherwise not many staff. Perhaps they were with Sarah and the doctor, which meant Doris was getting lots of attention. He wandered into the dining room and made his way over towards Alistair, who had given him some bacon yesterday. Perhaps he would give him some today. Alistair saw Howard coming towards him and smiled. He bent forward and stroked Howard's neck, casually dropping a small piece of bacon by his foot. Howard, seeing the doctor leaving, carried his bacon into the foyer and lay down in a band of sunlight. Slowly he ate the warm bacon, thinking how they could get their big adventure back on track. He needed to come up with an idea before Pierre and Olivia came back tonight and before Doris woke up. He would certainly feel much better if he could come up with a brilliant idea. All he had to do was think of one.

As he lay, looking out at the big wide world, his attention strayed from outside to what was happening inside. Humans walking along the corridors, chatting to each other, others looked at the same books he and Doris had looked at to get their adventure up and running and another was checking what events were happening in the centre for the next month. Slowly they moved off and the foyer became quiet again, so he got up and strolled around the foyer looking at the flowers and the posters on the board, carefully reading each one. There was so much going on; whist, keep fit, Skype (whatever that was), baking, a quiz, painting and a writing competition and then his eyes lit up. He turned and ran at full speed around the centre. Some humans were worried something had happened to him and tried to catch him, but they all failed because he was far too fast.

Chapter 5

Back On

Howard was so excited, he was totally unaware that Doris had just come out of Sarah's room and ran straight into her. Screeching and hissing, they rolled along the corridor, causing much amusement amongst the staff and residents. Both cats regained their dignity, brushed themselves down and strolled back to the foyer as if nothing had happened. Shaking their heads, the onlookers went back to what they had been doing. The adventurous pair settled down side by side in the sunlit foyer and Doris asked Howard if he was okay after his mad dash around the corridors as if his tail was on fire. Howard nodded and told Doris that the news on the big adventure had not been good.

Pierre and Olivia had reported back this morning and said there was no shortage of things they could use, but it was all too big for either of them to carry back, so they needed another plan.

Howard then went on to say that that was the reason for his mad moment, when he realised how they could do it.

"And how is that, then?" asked Doris.

"Simples," said Howard, (he had heard that on television from a talking Meerkat and found it funny). "We run a competition. Pierre and Olivia can put posters around the area asking people to build rockets, just like that programme I saw on television and we can use the best one to go on our adventure."

So it was decided they would run a competition, open to anyone of any age. They would ask all competitors to build a fully functional rocket that was capable of carrying up to 12 kg inside the main rocket: they could either design the rocket themselves or copy one they had already seen.

The prize, well they would become famous, but they would not know they were building a rocket to get the two adventurous cats into space.

Both laughed and both said, "Simples."

Now they just needed lots of posters to advertise the competition. Doris volunteered to do that tonight and after all the excitement they both catnapped once again, dreaming of space.

Exhausted with the near CATastrophic failure of their project before it had got off the ground so to speak, they woke up as it was getting dark again: but then, living this far up north, winter days were short, so they did not feel so bad about it. Once again their thoughts turned to planning, and what the wording would be on the posters. Thinking of what to put on the posters they both sensed they were being watched, and casually got up and walked towards the residents' lounge. Alistair and Sarah, who was now feeling better, were coming towards them. Alistair winked and Sarah smiled.

They were heading back to their bedrooms and sleep. As they passed Howard and Doris, they tried to bend down to stroke them but were not quite able to reach, so the caring cats jumped on to the arm of a chair, making it easier to be reached and stroked. Sarah gave them another beautiful smile and looked so much better since Doris had spent the night on her bed. Alistair winked again: They must know what we are up to, thought Howard, but how could they? As everyone made their way to their separate rooms and staff tidied up, Howard and Doris found a quiet spot behind the reception desk, this time hoping no one would see them there. They would listen carefully though for Pierre and Olivia. They lay there relaxing, now that the pressure for them to build a rocket had been taken off them, and chatted about what to put on the poster and after much thought they decided it would look like this:

Lochcarron Space Programme.
Are you interested?

We are looking for people who would like to design and build a space rocket. There are NO age limits, groups or individuals can enter.

You will need to build a working rocket/spaceship, which is propelled and is able to carry a minimum weight of 14kg. The prize will be life changing for the winner(s), who will not be announced until all the entries have been judged.

We would like all entries to be delivered and displayed at the library car park on Saturday 22nd June 2013, so that all contestants, members of the public and judges can see them. The initial flights will be at 1600 hrs at the Shinty field.

Best of luck to all the competitors
Sandra D. Howroid

Later, Howard and Doris decided to sit by the window and look up into the night sky, thinking of the weekend in June when all their planning came together and they could fulfil their dreams and go into space. They thought they had done rather well for two little cats from the Highlands of Scotland.

Doris saw something moving across the car park and tapped Howard's paw and pointed to where she had seen the movement. Across the car park came Pierre. Not too far behind was Olivia, zigzagging a silent path towards him. Neither seemed in a hurry as they probably thought there would be no trip to the moon, no cats in space, the end of the Lochcarron space programme and would have no idea that Howard had come up with a new idea.

The outsiders greeted the insiders with a silent "Hello" and said, "We have been thinking and talking about how to get all the equipment from the surrounding area, but realised we would need more help."

Howard said, "Don't worry, we have come up with a better idea and we can get the rocket built for us."

Olivia replied, "Now that is a good idea, but who will do that for you?" Doris answered. "We are going to run a competition where people design and build a rocket or spaceship that can fly and we use the best one for our adventure, but we need to put the posters up around the village and surrounding area. Would you do it, please?" Doris pleaded.

Pierre and Olivia agreed to help; it would be a lot easier than carrying everything else they would need to build their own rocket.

With that, Pierre and Olivia said they would be on their way for tonight and would call back tomorrow night and see if their adventurous friends had made any posters.

Doris said she would do a pretty poster on the computer, with pictures of the moon and rockets and then photocopy them in small batches, otherwise it might be found on the computer and their secret would be out.

They were not sure if Alistair or Sarah really knew or not, neither of them had said anything, just winked and smiled.

The outsiders set off on their nightly foray, Pierre trotting off towards Main Street and Olivia gliding low towards the medical centre, but just as she got to the road a car came screeching around the corner and she had to ascend very quickly. The car braked as she flew up over the windscreen, to the nearest tree to calm down. Poor Olivia was really shaken, her heart beat so fast and her breathing got faster too as she thought what might have happened if she had not been so quick. She decided there would be no hunting tonight, she would stay where she was and rest. This little owl did not want to die just yet.

Doris told Howard she would go and do the poster and would print just one copy and delete the file from the computer, so there would be no record of it. Next, she would photocopy 10 posters which Pierre and Olivia could distribute tomorrow night. She told Howard to go and have a good sleep as he had been very busy since they had started planning their adventure; she added, "I'm so proud of you."

Howard said, "I'm proud of you too, Doris. I think we have done rather well for two little cats from Lochcarron." With that he wandered off to find a nice comfortable chair to sleep on. Doris completed the poster, which looked very professional and then made 10 copies. She hid them where she hoped nobody would find them, and she went off to sleep on Sarah's bed again. She crept into the bedroom so as not to wake her and leapt onto the bed. Sarah wiggled and sighed but did not wake. Doris settled down and went off to sleep.

Chapter 6

Could Insiders Know?

Doris could not remember much of that night, she must have been exhausted, but woke up with a hand caressing her head and was convinced she heard Sarah say, "So our little cats are off to the moon, are they? I hope you are both kept safe," but Doris was not sure if she had actually heard it or dreamt it. You know how it is when you are waking up, sort of awake but not. Doris lifted her head and looked at the smiling Sarah, rolled over onto her back with her head in Sarah's hand and went back to sleep.

Young Howard had been having a lovely peaceful sleep, he had spent all night asleep in the armchair, stretched out as much as he could on his back, with his feet in the air, dreaming of himself and Doris flying off into space. He dreamt they had been to the moon and were just coming back to land on the shinty field when he woke up with a bang. He thought for a moment that the landing had gone badly wrong, but realised he had just rolled off the armchair and landed on the floor. He had come back to earth with a bang, but only from an armchair, not space, and he chuckled. After he regained his composure, he went off in search of his friend Doris, guessing she had finished the posters, but checked the computer and the photocopier just in case she had not. He thought for a minute and guessed she would probably be with Sarah, so he went to her bedroom and peered around the door and there was Doris, wide awake this time, being stroked by Sarah. He could hear Doris purring from the door. Doris saw Howard and stood up, stretching and waving her tail. She turned and looked at Sarah, took two steps and elegantly jumped off the bed. She and Howard walked back up the corridor to the foyer and once again sat by the window, looking out as a new day dawned and the daily routine got under way. Doris told Howard what she thought Sarah had said.

Howard was not sure about Sarah's remark to Doris. Had she really said it or had Doris dreamed it? They could never be sure and Howard had thought about stopping Doris from going to see Sarah, but at the very start of the adventure they said they must try to behave as normally as possible and not raise any suspicions. If they had, it was too late, but they were not going to stop now. Howard and Doris were too excited about their adventure now to worry too much about two humans possibly knowing about their secret. It was not as though anyone would believe them if they were told; who would believe that two cats could plan such an adventure and have got as far with it as well? Anyway, they did not care. All they had to do was produce some posters now and the people of Lochcarron and the surrounding area would build them a rocket. They had not given much thought to what they would do if nobody could build one for them, but they would have to cross that bridge when they came to it.

The lights around the centre flickered into life. The cats liked this time of day, as everyone wanted to make a fuss of them: the day staff as they arrived, the night staff as they went home and the residents as they pottered to and fro throughout the day. Today was going to be different, though, as they had no more planning to do, just print some posters for their outsider friends to put around the area. Otherwise all was back to normal, just normal everyday cats again, but not very exciting.

As the residents came through for breakfast, Doris decided she was going to stay where she was, hoping to keep out of the way, she was not too sure of Sarah at the moment. Howard thought he would go and get some bacon from Alistair this morning, as he had done most mornings, and he set off for the dining room, where Alistair sat in his usual place, eating his breakfast. Howard wandered around the table and chair legs until he arrived by Alistair, who as always, dropped a small piece of bacon. Howard looked at Alistair and lay down to eat it. Howard was now thinking of sleep again, and he decided to follow Alistair and curl up on his bed and dream of space. This time he hoped he would not end up on the floor, not good for a cat's credibility. As they went slowly through the foyer, Doris caught sight of them and ran over to see what was happening.

Howard said, "I'm just going for a sleep after my bacon."

Doris asked if she could come too. "It is easier to avoid humans if you are in someone's room," she said. Howard did not mind, so they all ambled along together.

When they got to Alistair's room, he opened the door for them. Howard and Doris ran in and jumped up on to the bed, but Doris landed on something hard and let out a squeal. Howard looked at her and what she had landed on. It was a pile of books, but not just any books. They were all the books that Howard and Doris had looked at for their big adventure. Stunned, both turned to look at Alistair, who was closing the door and he winked at the two of them. Alistair slowly walked over to his armchair and sat down, sighing a little. His joints were aching a bit today, but he was not getting any younger and his days of adventure were over now, but he liked adventures and was prepared to help the centre cats if he could. They looked up at him and then down at the books piled on the bed. Alistair had all of them, even the map they had used. This could not be just a coincidence and our two cats were worried that Alistair was going to stop their big adventure.

Chapter 7

Insiders Helping

Alistair coughed to clear his throat before speaking to his cat friends. "Well you two, it looks like someone is planning a bit of an adventure doesn't it?" Neither knew what to say and just sat there, unsure of what to do.

Alistair said, "Do not worry, we are not going to stop you, we will help you if we can."

"We?" blurted out Howard.

"Yes, we, both myself and Sarah. We know all about your plans for adventure, we can help if you would like us to, and your secret is safe with us."

Doris looked at Howard and shrugged her shoulders as if to say, "What do we do?"

Howard smiled and said, "It is okay, Doris. I trust my friend and I'm sure you trust yours, don't you?"

Doris nodded and then relaxed back on the bed, thinking how much fun it would be.

Alistair said he would arrange for Sarah to meet them in the residents' lounge later that day and discuss how they could help. He got up to open the door for them and said, "Off you go then and we will see you later."

In the excitement of getting some human help with their adventure, our two cats soon fell asleep in the foyer, having similar dreams of space rockets, trips to the moon and coming back to a very, very surprised Lochcarron village. If word got out, people would come for miles to see these two intrepid cats blast off into space from the Bealach Na Ba, but probably just as many people would turn up to stop it: SSPCA, Health and Safety Executive, Cats Protection League to name but a few. If they were going to do it on their own they could plead dumb and ignorant, how would cats know about such things as health and safety and such things? But now they had two human helpers, they could be in big trouble if it got out that two cats from the renowned Howard Doris care centre were going into space.

Howard rolled over in his sleep, hitting Doris on the head and waking her up. She was not happy and jabbed a sleeping Howard in the ribs with a claw. Doris told him to be more careful in future and went to get up. As she did so, she saw Alistair and Sarah coming up the corridor towards them. Doris hissed at Howard and he turned round to look and sprang to his feet excitedly. Their plan could really take off now and he chuckled; I'm so funny, he thought. The happy cats followed their friends into the lounge and sat on their knees. What was going to happen now, would it all turn out as they had planned?

Alistair spoke first. He said they had known the two little cats had been planning something for a while but only worked out what it was a few weeks ago, when he found one of the books they had left on the floor. "We saw you knock it from the shelf and push it to the window, and you both fell asleep with it open at rockets." The cats looked at each other. They could remember getting the book out but not falling asleep, surely not, they had tried so hard not to make it obvious and then they fell asleep reading a book, how stupid!

Alistair and Sarah asked how far they had got with their plans, and the cats told them they had outside help from a pine marten (Pierre) and a short eared owl (Olivia), and how they had planned to build a rocket themselves, but their friends could not carry all the parts back to the centre, so now they were going to run a competition and get the locals to build one for them. They explained how they thought it would work and showed them the poster which Doris had designed.

Sarah said, "There should be a contact telephone number for enquiries."

Alistair said, "Put mine and we can discuss what I need to say."

The cats agreed and it was decided they would keep the name Sandra D Howroid (an anagram of Howard and Doris) but use Alistair's number. He would just say Sandra was busy but he knew the rules and regulations, so could help with any questions.

Our cats went on to explain why the rockets and spaceships were to be put on display outside on the library car park and what was going to happen and when. Alistair and Sarah both smiled and started laughing and laughing until it hurt. They could not believe these cute little cats who had spent all their days in the centre had thought up this plan, and a second plan as well. They realised straight away that plan A would not work but plan B was brilliant and something the whole community of Lochcarron and surrounding areas could get involved in.

Howard said Pierre and Olivia would get the posters around the area.

Alistair said, "We can do some as well, we are going to Applecross next week and we could leave some over there, just lying around."

They all agreed that nobody else needed to know. It would be just Howard and Doris, their two outsider friends, Pierre and Olivia, and their two good friends, Alistair and Sarah. They could manage quite well on their own and most of the work had been done by the clever cats, all they had to do now was get the posters out, possibly field a few questions and then sit and wait for 22nd June and the adventure would really begin. Doris agreed to continue photocopying the posters, but would re-do them with a telephone number, just in case anybody needed to ask any questions. Alistair suggested they also printed an entry form. So it was decided Doris would design an entry form which could be collected from the library part of the Howard Doris centre and had to be returned on completion. Everyone agreed on the closing date for those wishing to enter as Saturday 17th February 2013.

Howard and Doris left their two friends and went back to sitting in the foyer. Both of them felt happy with what they had achieved so far, but Doris had a niggling thought about how all the humans would treat Alistair and Sarah if the adventure failed. Would their kind friends be held responsible? Doris told Howard of her fears and they agreed to go along that night to speak to them.

Chapter 8

Insiders' Stories

That evening they set off to see their two friends again to express their fears for them. As they walked along the corridors they occasionally stopped to be stroked or patted, by the residents, staff and visitors. Eventually they made it to Alistair's room and looked in through the partially opened door and saw him in his armchair with his head resting in his hands, crying! They looked at their sad friend and wondered what had happened to make him so sad. They ran over to him and brushed against him.

Doris asked, "What is the matter?"

Alistair said, "I'm just being silly. After we left you in the foyer we both said how happy we are that we can help you, but it could be our last adventure as we are both getting old now."

Both cats asked him not to cry, because they were happy to have the help but neither wanted their friends to get into trouble.

Alistair said if they got into trouble neither he nor Sarah would mind, but they were sure they would not get into too much trouble and were proud to be involved in the cats' adventures. "We will both be fine," he added.

Howard and Doris decided that they would spend the rest of the afternoon with Alistair. Hopefully this would be good for him, it would take his mind off being sad and they could spend the afternoon talking about the adventure that was ahead of them and all about the moon and rockets and they would listen to the adventures that Alistair had enjoyed through his long life. They had heard some of them before but were sure he would have new ones to tell and they would be happy to listen. Time flew by as Howard and Doris listened to Alistair's stories of his adventures as a young boy with his two brothers. He was the middle one, Ivor the eldest was killed during the war, but Graham was still alive and living in Ullapool; they did not see each other very much but met up for birthdays and Christmasses. Alistair wanted to be a vet when he left school, but had to stay on his family farm and help look after the animals. He did not mind too much because at least he was still looking after animals and he loved them all, that is how he knew the cats were up to something.

One of the staff members came in to see if Alistair was alright as he had missed the teatime meal. He did this quite often though, as his appetite was not very big these days. She stopped to talk for a while but saw that he was happy, he had Howard on his lap and was stroking his ears and Doris sat on the bed, eyes fixed on Alistair, both cats purring.

The lady said, "It sounds like they are talking to you, Alistair." He just smiled and thought, if only you knew.

The lady said, "Goodnight," and left.

Alistair was getting tired now and said he was going to bed.

Howard and Doris got up and said they would go and get the posters finished and the entry forms copied.

They were sure Pierre and Olivia would be back tonight and they could start putting the posters out around the area. The cats bid Alistair goodnight and went off running up the corridor, back to their favourite spot in the foyer.

They sat looking out of the window up at the night sky, which was very black with no moon, but they could see a few stars twinkling in the darkness which made it very pretty.

Doris said laughing "We can call one AliSTAR!" Howard liked to see his friend laughing, she had a funny laugh and it meant that she was happy.

"We can tell him in the morning," he said.

Howard saw Pierre and Olivia coming down Millbrae and guessed their friends had met up somewhere, they were early tonight as all the lights were still on in the centre, but Howard need not have worried as the pair disappeared through the doctors' car park and out towards Slumbay and hopefully, they would be back later.

Doris remarked that staying with Alistair had been a good idea and she thought they had cheered him up as he had enjoyed talking about his family and the farm he worked on. It was no wonder he loved cats. They could hear the humans moving around again, maybe the day staff were about to go home and the lights would start going out soon. Doris hoped so as she wanted to get busy on the new poster and some entry forms, the sooner they got the posters out, the sooner they would know if any rockets would be built and they could go into space.

The day staff said, "Goodnight," and the night staff started turning the lights off as they made their way along the corridors, popping into the rooms to make sure all the residents were fine and didn't need anything. Although the staff were kept busy during the night with tidying and washing up, ironing etc., they were always available if a resident pressed their alarm.

Our adventurous cats waited a while in case anybody came back to the foyer and caught the cats at the computer or with the books. When Doris thought it was safe, she started work on the new poster with all the details of where to get the entry forms, closing dates and telephone numbers etc. She printed one and then started on the entry forms, giving details of what was wanted, where judging would take place. There would be no entry fee, but donations could be made to the Howard Doris Centre.

Chapter 9

Getting the Posters Out

As Doris finished photocopying the entry forms, Howard called her over. Their two outsider friends were coming back across the car park, they could now start getting the posters out around the area. Pierre and Olivia would be busy tonight, but they did not know it yet. Their two friends arrived at the little open window as they usually did and Olivia perched on the windowsill, while Pierre stood up on his hind legs and held on to the windowsill with his front paws. They wanted to know how the plans were going.

Howard said they had been busy with their two insider friends who now knew the cats were planning something, but had not quite imagined two cats going into space, but had been very helpful and would now do what they could to help. Howard explained there would now be six of them involved in the space programme and Alistair and Sarah would help deliver posters further out of the area. Pierre and Olivia said that would be helpful because both of them had to catch food and eat as well as deliver posters.

"Have you got some to deliver tonight?" asked Olivia.

"Yes, we have," came the instant reply from Doris.

The four friends spent an hour talking about the adventure and how planning was going well, especially now they had two insider humans helping them.

Olivia said "I could not ever imagine going up into space," she added. "I get giddy sometimes now if I fly too high."

The others laughed, as they never realised birds could get giddy. Olivia was not amused, and asked for some posters to take and she was gone.

"Oh dear," said the others. "Perhaps we should not have laughed."

Pierre grabbed some posters and went off after her. Our two cats were a bit sad now, Olivia had rushed off upset because they had laughed at her and then Pierre had rushed after her, leaving Howard and Doris alone. All was quiet now as the residents had gone to bed. They could still hear the staff moving around and talking, but they rarely came up to the foyer at night. Howard and Doris decided they would have to come up with a plan to get the rocket up to the top of the Bealach Na Ba, so they sat by their favourite spot discussing ideas, but it was difficult for two little cats who did not know very much about the outside world. The hours ticked by on the foyer clock. Every second seemed to echo around the centre, making it harder to think of a purrfect plan. Eventually they decided they would have to ask their two friendly insiders for help on that one, as the only person they knew that had driven up to it was Dr Murray when the staff did a moonlight walk. Dr Murray would be shocked if a cat started talking to him. It could also mean the end of their adventure, with another human knowing their plans: after all, the fewer humans that knew the better it was for all concerned, so they did what cats do best and went to sleep. Our two sleepy cats eventually woke up about 0430 hrs and had a good stretch and a wash, then lay by the window again looking out across the darkness to the mountains and sky beyond, wondering how many rockets could be lined up outside on 22nd June, but more importantly, how good they would be? Doris saw two shadows approaching the window, it was Pierre and Olivia. Olivia gently landed on the windowsill and before she had got herself comfortable, both cats said, "Sorry we laughed at you, it was thoughtless of us." Olivia tutted, got herself comfortable and said, "It's okay. I should not have got upset I was a bit sensitive about my flying, but I am only young and am still learning really."

Everyone was friends again and Pierre and Olivia said they had put the posters around Lochcarron. Pierre had been putting his through people's letter boxes and Olivia leaving hers in porches if the doors were open, or on doorsteps and hoping it did not rain. Both said they would be back tonight for some more and disappeared into the darkness again. The cats were pleased that they were all friends again and stayed looking out of the window. As soon as the lights went on they would go and meet Alistair and Sarah, hopefully the humans could work out how to get a rocket and the two cats up to the top of the Bealach Na Ba without anyone getting suspicious.

Chapter 10

Up the Bealach Na Ba

They saw several car headlights coming along the road and yellow flashing lights flicking on and off, as each car in turn headed down Millbrae and stopped in the very car park which would hold all the space rockets. The night staff got out and walked and talked as they came towards the foyer and the cats got up to welcome them. As the doors opened the lights flickered into life, stinging the little cats' eyes because of the brightness. Howard bumped into Doris because he could not see her but said, "Sorry!" straight away and stood perfectly still until his eyes got used to the lights, then carried on making a fuss of the staff and they did the same to him and Doris.

As soon as things calmed down, Howard and Doris went to see Alistair and Sarah. Each went to see their own friend and asked them if they could think of a way to get a rocket and two cats up to the top of the mountain. They asked if they could meet in the residents' lounge after lunch and all agreed, that would give them time to come up with a plan. Howard walked back to the dining room with Alistair, thinking of his stomach as usual. If any cat was heading for heart problems it was Howard, perhaps he should get a health check before doing something as adventurous as going into space. He would discuss it with Doris later. "Once I have had my bacon," he laughed to himself. Later in the day, Howard and Doris met up with their human friends, to come up with a plan to get the two cats in a position to be launched into space. They met up in the residents' lounge, where it was always quiet after lunch and all had time to think of possible ideas. So far only Sarah had come up with what seemed a perfectly good idea. She sat in the armchair, smiling as she always did, and leaned forward, resting her chin on a delicate little hand with perfectly painted nails. She cleared her throat and began to explain her plan, which sounded quite simple.

"As you are getting all the rockets on to the car park overnight so the judges and public can see them all, we need to choose the one we think is best and just before it gets light on the Sunday morning, we put you two adventurous cats into the capsule.

"Next, instead of us having to get rockets up to the top of the Bealach Na Ba, we ask all the contestants to collect them from the car park and take them up themselves to launch, and we can have each launch in turn. When the rockets are still in the car park, Alistair can re-wire the controls so that he has control rather than the owners, as I know he used to build his own model aircraft in his younger days."

"That is an excellent idea," Alistair said, "What do you cats think of that?

The cats thought for a moment and then huddled together to discuss it. Eventually they sat up and said, "We are quite happy with the idea as long as Alistair is able to re-wire the rocket."

Alistair said he would be able to and would start work tomorrow. He would ask his friend in Inverness to get him the parts he would need. So it was decided. Everything was now organised, they would continue getting posters out and could actually see if people took application forms as they were in the foyer, then all they had to do was wait until the 22nd June, which seemed an awful long way off.

Chapter 11

It's Happening!

Doris was looking out of the residents' lounge when she saw a lot of activity in the foyer close to where the library books were kept, so she jumped up and went to see what was going on. As she got to the door she could see a group of adult humans and some not-so-big humans. Doris guessed these must be the teenagers they had heard so much about. What were they doing? She wondered, but as she got closer she could see they had all picked up entry forms. Excited, she turned to run back to her friends when BANG! The door had closed behind her. One of the teenagers came to see what had happened and was just in time to see poor Doris get up to her feet and shake herself down. He bent down to stroke her and let her through the door. Doris was embarrassed as she made her way back to the others but none of them laughed or mentioned it, they just wanted to know what was happening in the foyer.

Doris was so excited and kept saying again and again, "It's happening, it's happening." That was until Howard shouted, "*What* is happening"?

Doris went quiet now and said, "All those people were collecting entry forms, most of them have gone. We are going into space, Howard, we really are."

Alistair tried to calm things down and eventually Doris calmed down.

"Yes, people have got entry forms and yes, some of them might build a rocket, but it does not mean it will be good enough to take you and Howard into space, for that we will have to wait and see," said Alistair.

The days were still short up here in the Highlands, but life was more relaxed and people had time to speak to each other. Alistair and Sarah said it was not like that in the cities. Neither Howard nor Doris wanted to be city cats, where the thought of being hit by a car or catnapped was very worrying. Everyone looked forward to the longer days of summer and hoped they would have another good one like last year and spend their days lying in the sun by the windows.

"Aah" sighed Doris. It was getting dark again, although the nights were getting shorter. Pierre and Olivia still had plenty of time to deliver more posters. Those that had been given out so far had got people interested. Hopefully, more would take part and Lochcarron really would have a good space programme. Howard thought it might become an annual event as more people from further away might take part. They could go into space every year if they wanted to, or let other cats or animals go instead. Howard's mind was becoming over-active now and Doris told him not to get too excited as they might not even get into space this year. Hadn't he been listening to Alistair earlier? Howard got up and walked to the window. Doris followed although she was not sure if she had upset Howard or not. As it turned out he had only wanted to be by the window, looking outside at the moon at night and sometimes he could see it during the day. Even though Howard and Doris were hoping to go into space, there were a lot of things our little cats did not know. It was not long before Pierre and Olivia came to visit. They approached from opposite directions and almost arrived together. Olivia just ahead of Pierre, was making herself comfortable on the window sill as Pierre came around the corner of the library.

They all said, "Hello" before discussing how things were progressing.

"We have had lots of entry forms taken today," said Doris and asked if Olivia and Pierre could take some more posters with them.

"I am more than happy to take some as I am going up to Kirkton Woods tonight, so I will deliver around Kirkton Road and Sage Terrace."

Olivia said, "I'm going hunting around the fields on Croft Road, so I will do that area."

Doris handed them as many posters as each of them could carry and off they went. Pierre offered Olivia a ride on his back, as long as she did not dig her claws in. Olivia climbed on to Pierre's back and went off into the darkness, chatting as they went. Pierre kept to the shadows and backs of the houses so they were not seen. As they approached the shore side opposite the Waterside café, there was little cover.

Pierre told Olivia, "Hold on tight," and sprinted across the road, making their way towards the old service point office and up the footpath to Croft Road, from there they went their separate ways.

Chapter 12

Time Goes Slowly

Howard was a bit disappointed now, because he realised he had nothing else to do until it was actually time to go up into space. Pierre and Olivia were going around at night delivering posters around the area. Alistair was building new controls for the prize winning rocket; he and Sarah were putting posters out when they went on their trips with the centre and Doris was still printing posters and entry forms. Howard thought of just going to sleep and leaving Doris with her jobs, but decided it was only fair to sit up with her and just look at the stars that twinkled in the darkness, wondering if there might be anything else out there that they could not see. Doris was already worried when the moon disappeared behind a cloud. If he started worrying about what he could not see, this space rocket could have two scaredy-cats on board. Doris photocopied 20 more posters and entry forms and put them on the library table and hid the posters for Pierre and Olivia to do another delivery, then sat down with Howard.

As she sat down, she asked Howard, "What are you thinking about?"

"Oh, nothing really. I am just looking up at the stars and wondering how far away they are." He did not mention what else might be up there waiting for them.

They both thought this was an ideal time for a sleep, and curled up together by the desk where it was nice and warm, Howard stretched out on his back as he liked sleeping that way and Doris just curled up around him as best she could and fell asleep. The cats slept deeply, worn out by their activities and were woken up by bright lights being turned on to welcome a new day. As their eyes got used to the lights, Howard rolled over and gave a big stretch to loosen his joints, Doris went to sit but flopped to the floor. Howard looked over at her, surprised, but Doris was okay.

"My paw has gone to sleep, but I'll be fine in a minute or two," she said. Doris sat looking out of the window, watching humans walking along the road and vehicles going past. 'I wonder if any of those humans will be building space rockets,' she thought. Howard joined her and both of them sat waiting for the day staff to get to work. They liked this time of day as they got lots of petting from staff coming and going, and Howard was thinking of his bacon treat. Doris looked down the corridor to see who was coming and thought she could hear Sarah and Alistair talking. Alistair and Sarah waved and came across to see them.

Sarah bent down and whispered to Doris, "How are the plans going?"

Doris purred and said, "Very well, thank you. Pierre and Olivia took some posters along to Kirkton and Croft Road, so hopefully more people will come today and get entry forms."

"That is good," said Sarah. "Alistair and I are really excited now, it is good we have something to look forward to."

Chapter 13

Doris Gets Upset

Alistair set off for the dining room. He, like Howard, had food on his mind and not much was going to stop him as he headed for his favourite chair. Howard ran up beside him, thinking, 'Why should I wait for him to call me, this saves me valuable eating time.' Howard jumped onto Alistair's lap and sat waiting for the lady to bring Alistair's breakfast. Today he was having bacon, sausage, egg, beans and toast, Howard could smell it already and started to drool on Alistair's trousers. Alistair pushed Howard off, he did not want his smart trousers covered in cat drool, but Howard still got his piece of bacon.

Alistair leant over Howard and whispered, "Could you and Doris come to my room after lunch? I have something to tell you both."

Howard said, "We will both be there," and he ran through to tell Doris. Doris was on the reception desk being stroked by Sarah, they both looked at Howard, who quickly ran behind the desk and leapt on to a chair and then on to the desk.

Sarah asked if he had got his bacon from Alistair.

He purred and said, "Yes."

"Did he tell you he would like to see you both after lunch?"

Again Howard purred. "Yes, I have just come to tell you, Doris, do you know why?"

Sarah smiled, then laughed. "You will have to wait and see." The cats watched her as she disappeared through the doors for her breakfast. Doris said quietly, "I wonder what they want us for, I hope they don't say they cannot help any more, that would be so unfair after we have got this far."

Howard said, "I don't think they would, but we will have to wait and see."

Doris jumped down and started pacing around the foyer, she was anxious now and desperately wanted to know what was happening. What was Alistair going to tell them? She paced up and down the foyer, tutting as she went. Howard was getting annoyed with her. He was, he admitted, a bit more laid back than Doris but her persistent tutting was getting to him and he jumped down in front of her as she passed.

"Doris, try to calm down and relax. You will make yourself ill and I might have to go into space on my own. Let us sit by the window and look outside and talk about the adventure." She quietly agreed and they settled down behind the books and watched the humans coming and going.

Howard purred, "Did you know at least 15 more humans have collected entry forms?"

Howard again asked Doris to calm down but she blamed him this time.

"I was all right until you said more humans had collected entry forms. That means more rockets and it might get cancelled, all our hard work for nothing." She sat down and cried. Sarah and Alistair came out of the dining room and saw Doris crying behind the books. They came over and Howard explained that Doris was worried that they were going to cancel their adventure.

Alistair said, "If you come back to my room now, I will tell you that we are not going to stop helping with your adventure."

Howard and Doris set off with their friends and settled down on the bed between them. Sarah curled her hand under Doris's chin and looked deep into her eyes and said, "Listen to Alistair, but do not worry your pretty little heads, everything will be fine." Alistair got up and moved to his comfy armchair. He could see them better from there, and said, "I am sorry I caused you to cry Doris, I never meant to. You see if we could have waited until this afternoon, I would have been able to show you, but instead I shall tell you. My friend from Inverness was coming over later this morning with the things I need to build my control panel and box, the next stage in your big adventure."

Doris was so pleased she leapt straight from the bed onto Alistair's lap and then started to lick his face with her little raspy tongue. Alistair laughed and told her to calm down.

Howard said, "I have been telling her to do that all morning and she never listened to me, either," They all laughed together, a happy little group of friends. Howard sat on the bed, thinking about Pierre and Olivia, who were also doing a lot of work for the Lochcarron space programme, but they would never be able to share what Howard and Doris would. He would ask them tonight if they were okay and show them that they cared about them too. He jumped from the bed and as he went through the doorway.

He turned and said "Thank you," to his three friends.

He was happy now, but did not want his friends to know he was just as worried about the space programme being cancelled as Doris was. He was just braver, he thought to himself, now he could sleep for a while and dream of stars, rockets and the moon.

It was well after lunch when Howard and Doris woke up. Howard woke first and stretched out as far as he could to ease his little joints and then rubbed his sleepy eyes, as he focused on the things around him. He noticed everything outside was getting battered by strong winds and lots and lots of rain, the trees bending so much he thought they might break and all around the building outside was a loud whistling noise. He went over to Doris who had gone to sleep on the receptionist's chair, purring with pleasure, and told her to come to the window and look outside. As they got to the door they heard a tapping outside, they got closer and closer, unsure of what it might be, both of them trying to be brave but also ready to run if it scared them. Howard carefully stretched up so that he could see over the panel, but did not jump as it was only a plastic bottle blowing in the wind.

Chapter 14

The Planning Comes Together

The two cats went off to see their two human friends, as Howard had said Alistair should have the parts for the control box and panel by now and he wanted to see what his friends had been talking about.

"To be honest," he said, "I had no idea what the two of them had been talking about. If I see it I might understand eventually, but after all I am only a cat, I don't know anything about flying yet."

Entering Alistair's room, they saw him in his armchair, at a little table covered in all sorts of bits and pieces.

Doris said, "That must be the control panel and control box."

Howard replied, "That's only two things and there are a lot more than two bits on the table, perhaps it got broken on the way here. I'm sure Alistair can rebuild it."

They made their way over to where Alistair was sitting and looked up at him as he pushed the table away and tapped his leg with a finger, to let them know that they could jump up. They both leapt up and settled down on his lap. Alistair told them how he was going to use all these parts to make their rocket fly into space. Doris started laughing but Howard and Alistair looked at her.

"What's so funny, Doris?" asked Howard.

"When I saw all those bits I thought it was broken," said Doris demurely. Now that everything had been explained to them, the cats set off for their favourite spot in the foyer.

It was still very windy outside but Howard had noticed that most of the entry forms had gone again, things were really looking promising for their adventure and Pierre and Olivia would be back tonight for some more posters. It was starting to get dark again and a bit scary, with that wind whistling and things banging and getting blown about. You could not really see what was happening and then something would fly past the door or bang against the window or wall, making Doris and Howard jump.

The daily routine of centre life was continuing as it always did and the night staff had come in and were busy checking on the residents. There was no commotion tonight, so all was well and the lights started clicking off, all but one in the foyer. It was flashing on and off like a warning light. Doris hoped everything would be okay, she was a right little worrier, was Doris.

As it got darker, Howard and Doris kept a lookout for Pierre and Olivia. Though it was still very windy, the little cats hoped that their friends would come for more posters. The rain eventually stopped and Pierre came trotting across the car park, rather muddy and not his usual clean self. They asked him if he had seen Olivia as she had not been round to see them.

"Since you have both been helping us you have always met up somewhere and come to see us together," said Doris.

Pierre replied that he had been to see Olivia on his way here, but she was not at home. He went on to say, laughing,

"I saw her walking up the path back towards her nest, apparently she went hunting and got blown away by the wind, so she decided to walk back and not go out again."

"Poor Olivia," they all said.

Howard informed Pierre that tonight would be the last night of poster deliveries for him, as Alistair and Sarah were going out on a day trip. Tomorrow they would be going to Sheildaig, Applecross, Torridon, Kinlochewe and Gairloch, so they would put some posters out over there.

Doris said, "43 entry forms have been collected so far, thanks to you and Olivia."

Pierre was pleased and said he would take some more, now it had stopped raining. He laughed and said, "With this wind they might get blown miles away to foreign countries, then we might get international rockets to take you on your adventure."

Pierre set off towards Colonel's Road, stopping just long enough on the kerb to avoid being hit by a car. He was pleased with himself for being able to help his insider friends plan their space adventure and hoped they would be safe on their journey and return to Lochcarron.

After Pierre left, Doris set about photocopying 30 final posters. Alistair and Sarah would put these out on their day trip tomorrow and hopefully, a lot more entry forms would be collected and there would be lots of space rockets brought along for the competition on the 22nd June.

When Doris finished the posters, they chatted for a while about the big adventure they had planned and all the help their good friends had given them. Afterwards they cuddled up and went to sleep by the window, with the stars twinkling in the dark sky and thoughts of space travel on their minds.

Chapter 15

No Day Trip for Alistair

They eventually woke up with the day staff arriving and discussing what, if anything had happened during the night. Doris heard a member of staff mention Alistair's name, saying he had not gone to bed last night, just sat in his armchair making something.

Doris smiled and thought, 'well done, Alistair,' but when she told Howard he was angry and said he would go and see Alistair.

He went running along the corridor and Doris set off behind him trying to keep up. Why was Howard so angry? Doris thought. They got to Alistair's room and saw him fast asleep in his armchair.

Howard shook his head and said to Doris, "We will let him sleep now but I will come back later and tell him that he must go to bed and not stay up building things for us. We do not want him to get ill."

On the way back along the corridor they called in to see Sarah and told her what Alistair had been doing. She was not happy about it either, but told the little cats not to worry, she would have a word with him and stop him from doing it again. Nobody wanted him losing sleep and possibly getting ill. As it was he probably would not make the day trip today. Sarah said she would take the posters anyway. The cats walked along the corridor with Sarah as she went for breakfast, she looked really lovely all done up in her best clothes ready for her day out, and they hoped Alistair could make it because he was really looking forward to it. Howard felt guilty as it was because of them he had not slept and would probably miss the day out.

Howard was feeling sad now and did not fancy any bacon today, although his friend was not there to give it to him anyway. The pair sat down in the foyer looking through the window at the people who were coming in and out of the foyer and leaving paper by the library computer. Doris got up and jumped onto the computer desk to have a look at where they were all laid neatly on top of each other and suddenly realised they were entry forms that had been returned.

She jumped down and ran over to Howard to tell him and he jumped up excitedly and shouted in cat speak, "Humans are building us rockets, we will be going into space, yippee!"

Our two adventurous cats were really excited now. All their months of planning and now, thanks to all their friends, well four friends, it looked like all the hard work was going to be worth it and the Lochcarron space programme would be officially launched on 22nd June 2013.

As the closing date for entries neared, more entry forms had been returned, 37 at the last count and the posters Sarah had left at Sheildaig, Applecross, Torridon, Kinlochewe and Gairloch on her trip out had brought lots more new entries in. Now Howard and Doris and their two friends had to plan what was going to happen and how. They met in the lounge and Howard suggested they have two flights from each rocket, from the Shinty field with the builders taking charge of liftoff and landings. This would give Alistair the chance to choose the best one and when all the rockets were taken to the library car park for the night, Alistair could re-wire the best one so he could take control of it and put the cats on board. On Sunday 23rd June they could launch them one by one from the Bealach Na Ba.

Alistair said "I think we should pick the best 10 rockets and just launch those from the Bealach Na Ba, or we could be there for a very long, cold night."

So it was agreed that they had an excellent plan and that was how they could get Howard and Doris up into space.

There were only three more days before the closing date. Alistair had almost finished the control panel and box and calculated that if a rocket was to be able to carry a maximum load of 14kg, it would have to be a minimum size, but his control panel would certainly fit this minimum size and allow Howard and Doris room to be comfortable as well.

Chapter 16

Time Goes Slowly

The excitement of planning their big adventure was over and the cats missed getting the posters and entry forms photocopied, and sitting around waiting for Pierre and Olivia to come round to collect them for delivery. They missed telling them about their plans. Their two outsider friends still came round to see them most nights and always asked how the big adventure was going, but life was rather dull. If they felt like this now, what would it be like when the whole adventure was over and they returned to normal everyday cat lives? Could they cope with that or would they need an even bigger adventure? There was nothing our cats could do now apart from normal everyday cat things, whiling away the final few days until the closing date, when the ultimate 'cats in space' adventure could begin. Both cats realised that just because some people had entered their rockets into the programme, it did not mean any of them would be good enough to take them into space, and they would not know until each competitor had flown their initial flight on the 22nd June.

The closing date for all entries arrived and Howard and Doris went to meet up with Alistair and Sarah in the lounge. Their friends were sitting on the sofa, with a pile of papers on the coffee table. The excited cats ran across to see them and rubbed against the legs of their friends. Alistair bent down to pick Howard up and groaned a bit as he did so: his bones ached and Howard was a bit of a heavy cat to lift. Doris jumped up beside Sarah and settled on her knees.

Sarah picked up the pile of papers and waved them in the air with a happy smile "Well, you intrepid little Lochcarron cats, we have a grand total of 43 rocket entries, from as far away as Broadford and Gairloch, so hopefully we will get a suitable rocket for your adventure."

Alistair said, "I have finished the control box and control panel and it will be easy to fit it into the best rocket or spaceship we can find." He added, "I think both cats should get a health check before they go into space, to be sure they are fit enough."

Doris laughed and said, "Of course we are fit enough, neither of us have ever been ill, but we will do it anyway, especially Howard with his liking for bacon."

So it was decided that both cats would have a bout of sneezing so they could be taken to the vet's and checked out for any illnesses or diseases. Doris did not like needles but she was prepared to do it for the good of the Lochcarron space programme. Alistair's idea, to sprinkle pepper where they usually slept, made them sneeze and their eyes water continually. So the cats were bundled into cat carriers and driven over to the vets in Dingwall. When the lady vet saw them they weren't sneezing anymore and the amazed staff members apologised saying, "It stopped suddenly."

The vet said, "Well, as they are both here now I may as well give them a check over." So each of them got a thorough examination, including their temperature taken.

Neither of them liked that bit at all, but it was worth it to be passed as fit. "Both cats are fighting fit," were the words the vet used, which puzzled the cats because they had no plans to fight, they only wanted to fly into space.

When they arrived back at the centre, they ran to find their two special friends and tell them that although the examination by the vet hadn't been fun, they had both been passed as fully fit and would be able to go into space as they had hoped and planned. Their adventure was now able to start properly and everything had been prepared so they just had to sit and wait until the 22nd June came around. From the closing date to the preliminary flights, time seemed to go very, very slowly. Howard and Doris wished they had something other than everyday cat things to do, but all they had was eating, sleeping and being stroked: all very nice if you are a normal cat, but they did not see themselves as normal cats any more, they were Lochcarron space cats. After what seemed an eternity, the day before the big day arrived and started as every day had for as long as they could remember. Howard went through his normal routine of waking up and having a big stretch to loosen his joints, then he and Doris ran excitedly down the corridor to see Alistair and Sarah. As they arrived at Alistair's room, they could see him in his armchair, talking to somebody and playing with the control box that he had so kindly assembled for them. Howard and Doris could hear the control panel making a whirring noise and see bits moving up and down. Alistair was having a final test run and all was working properly. They strolled in and saw Sarah sat on the bed chatting away to Alistair. She stopped when she saw them and welcomed the little space cats with a smile.

"Well you two, tomorrow is your big day. When all the spaceships and rockets arrive today Alistair and I will go to the shinty field and find our little friends the best one for their adventure."

Alistair put the control box down and said, "It is working perfectly, I will hide everything away and we can go to breakfast."

"Mmmm," said Howard.

Doris laughed and said, "You and your bacon, Howard! You had better not eat too much or the rocket might not lift us off the ground."

In the dining room Alistair leant over to give Howard his bacon treat and whispered, "You and Doris come to my room after tea tonight and we will finalise the plans for tomorrow. Get as much sleep as possible because you will be up in space tomorrow and probably too excited to sleep properly."

Howard said, "When I have finished my treat Doris and I will curl up by the books and dream about tomorrow."

Chapter 17

Practice Day Arrives

Howard and Doris were just getting comfortable when a car arrived in the car park. It was towing a trailer with a rocket on it which looked rather big and impressive, but they did not know much about rockets. They decided not to sleep but just sit and watch the rockets arriving, as they could always sleep tonight. More rockets arrived, all shapes and sizes and the people that built them set them up in the car park for judging. They saw Alistair and Sarah go outside and start talking to the people. Howard and Doris guessed they were letting them know what was going to happen over the weekend: that is, apart from two cats being launched into space. Alistair and Sarah came back and sat on the bench outside, looking at the rockets as they arrived.

Howard said to Doris, "Next time the door opens, shall we run out and sit with them?"

Doris agreed and it wasn't long before the doors opened again and they ran out into the big wide world and lay down under their friends' bench, where they felt safe.

The car park was slowly filling up with rockets and spaceships and people were walking around looking at them. As each one arrived, their two friends walked over and spoke to them and then came back to the bench. The staff came out and asked what they were doing. Alistair explained that it was he and Sarah who had organised this event, to give the locals a project that they could all get involved in. The staff were surprised, but did not try to stop them. They said they would be happy to sell tea, coffee, cakes and biscuits to those that wanted them, and wished them well. By 1600 hrs (4pm) all entries had arrived at the car park and all had been admired by fellow contestants and passers-by alike. Alistair and Sarah walked around the spaceships and rockets a number of times and liked what they saw; they were suitably impressed with the first ever Lochcarron space programme entries. Alistair stood up and asked for quiet, the noise slowly subsided and all was peaceful apart from the occasional bird singing in the hedges. He thanked all the people who had taken the time to build each rocket and all the people who had come to have a look. He said, "I hope that everyone will have a very enjoyable weekend and all being well, this will be the first of many annual Lochcarron space programme events." He requested that all contestants take their craft along to the shinty field, where preparations for the first test flights would take place.

As the humans arrived at the shinty field, they were surprised to see a fête laid on as well, with lots of stalls around the outside of the fence and all funds going to the Howard Doris centre. The fire service and ambulance service were there just in case of accidents. Alistair and Sarah had been busy. The contestants gathered in the middle and each was asked to pick a number out of Alistair's hat. This would be the order in which the contestants launched their rockets and everyone wondered who would be the first one to go. It did not take long for the draw to take place and Alistair let Sarah take over now. She spoke very clearly into the microphone as she welcomed everyone to the Lochcarron space programme and fête, wishing all those taking part the best of luck and hoped the onlookers would enjoy a good evening. She wanted to thank Howard and Doris for coming up with this amazing idea but knew that she couldn't.

Chapter 18

The Lochcarron Space Programme

Launches

The first contestants nervously took their place at the launch pad and prepared for launch. It was a family effort and the little girl pressed the red button, held firmly by her dad and the rocket shot up into the air, going up about 250 metres before slowly drifting back to earth on a parachute. Everyone cheered and clapped as the little girl jumped up and down excitedly. Alistair thought, 'this is going to be a good day'. As each contestant took their turn, some with more success than others, the first failure happened. Contestant number 13, who by coincidence had named his rocket Apollo 13, was obviously not at all superstitious. Built by a Gairloch schoolboy, it had a perfect launch and rose really fast but as it did so, it fell to pieces and dropped to the ground nearly as quickly as it had gone up. Everyone went, "Aaaaw," together, but applauded his efforts. The boy was upset, but tried not to show it and some friends and strangers came to help him collect the pieces. Sarah put the microphone to her mouth and thanked the boy for his efforts and later gave him a special prize of £10 for his attempt. Only she and Alistair knew this was from her own money as there were no actual prizes, just a fun weekend and two adventurous cats hopefully going into space. More rockets and spacecraft were launched and came back to earth, some remote controlled, others like huge fireworks. One had caught the eye of Alistair and Sarah, and it was a model of the space shuttle built by some of the Lochcarron Garage workers. They hoped that it would fly as well as it looked, and it was the next one up. The garage staff pushed their own big launch ramp across to the centre of the field and pointed it towards the loch, while five other people carried the shuttle model over to it. This was the largest entry so far, it was at least two metres in length and certainly big enough to carry two cats. It was carefully positioned for launch and everyone stood well clear as flame issued from the rear of the shuttle and moved it along the launch ramp, where it quickly gathered speed and roared off. This shuttle was fast, faster and smoother than any of the others and it was over the loch and higher than Cnoc nam Mult, before it headed towards Attadale and Strathcarron and made a wide sweep over Tullich before heading high into the sky and over the mountains beyond. Alistair smiled and decided this was the one. They saw it glint in the sun as it turned and headed down towards Stromemore, across the loch and towards Ardnaff, where it soared high into the sky and out of sight. The shuttle came back into view as it plummeted earthwards and levelled out, skimming above the loch towards the avalanche shelter before it turned and headed back to the shinty field for a bumpy, but almost perfect landing. Every person who was there screamed, shouted and applauded this incredible machine. Alistair and Sarah looked at each other and smiled, this would be the one. 'Mission accomplished,' they thought.

The final five rockets took their turns but already they could not compete with the Lochcarron Garage space shuttle. Only one came very close, this was designed by Plockton High School and the flight was perfect, all beautifully controlled, but sadly landed badly and exploded when it hit the ground. The pupils were heartbroken but received cheers from the spectators and given an honorary second place. Alistair and Sarah brought the day's Lochcarron space programme to a close. They thanked everyone who had taken time to build a spacecraft and giving such enthusiastic support to the Lochcarron area. Sarah told them to enjoy the stalls as they had all given their time for free, as well as their takings to the Howard Doris Centre. She handed the microphone to Alistair, who informed them that tomorrow evening the nine best craft would be launched from the summit of the Bealach Na Ba. The launch would take place at 2200 hrs (10pm), just as the light was starting to fade, but there would be a full moon to give the space programme that special effect. Someone in the crowd shouted "Why are there only nine spacecraft?"

Alistair replied, "The Plockton School would have made it 10 but they cannot fly tomorrow, as it would be hard on them to send a replacement, so nine it will be and we would like to see everyone on the Bealach tomorrow night, but in the meantime all craft can be left in the car park, where they will be safe." The humans wandered around the field, having goes on the stalls, buying sweets, cakes and jams and the little humans were having fun on the rides and eating toffee apples and candy floss. Everyone was having a great afternoon, talking about spacecraft and speaking to those who had built them. As the evening got darker the humans made their way home, stalls closed up and the spacecraft were taken back to the car park. There was excitement in the village and Alistair and Sarah strolled home to tell the cats what had happened that afternoon. As they walked across the car park, Howard and

Doris saw them from the window and ran out the door to meet them. Howard nearly got run over by a trailer, luckily the big 4x4 managed to stop in time or the space programme would be over. They all walked back together and went into the lounge where Alistair and Sarah gave the cats a full rundown of the afternoon's events and how they had found the perfect space shuttle for them. They were very excited, but a little bit scared, too.

Chapter 19

Getting Ready to Go

Before he retired for the night, Alistair told Howard and Doris to get some sleep and he would get up at dawn and swap the control panel in the shuttle, then fetch the two of them and pack them safely, with a harness each and some food and water, so that they would be okay for their adventure.

Next morning, the alarm clock rang and a bleary-eyed Alistair awoke. It was a long time since he had been up at this time of the morning, but he had promised the cats and he always kept his promise. He slid out of bed and got dressed, but didn't bother to wash or shave, he could do that later, for he had far more important things to do. He packed a holdall with the control panel, box and a little video camera which would record the cats in space, then set off towards the foyer, feeling like a spy as he crept along the corridors and headed out towards the car park. Luckily no staff member saw him as he headed for the shuttle and he had to get busy, as there was quite a bit to do and he did not want to get caught. Alistair set to work, carefully unscrewing the cockpit hood and removing the wiring.

"It is easier than I thought it would be," he said to himself.

A voice replied, "I'm pleased about that."

He jumped back, nearly falling over, and realised it was Sarah who had come to keep him company. He looked down and she smiled at him as only she could.

Alistair went back to work, pleased his friend had come to keep him company. She did not speak, she just watched him working, happy with what he was doing and it was not long before he had replaced the control panel and reconnected the wiring. He just had to turn his control box on and make sure he was in control of it. He flicked a switch and the lights glowed as he slowly moved the levers; the left one up and down; the right one left and right and the middle one to control the speed. He smiled and nodded and Sarah knew everything was okay. Next, he secured two harnesses side by side, so the adventurous cats could see out if they wanted too but more importantly, see each other, then finally he attached the small video camera to prove the cats had actually flown. Time was getting on, so he packed his tools away and went to fetch the cats and some food and water. He made them safe in their harnesses and he and Sarah gave the cats a good luck kiss before sealing them in. They wished the little cats a safe journey and said, "We will see you again soon."

Walking back to the centre, Alistair glanced at his friend and saw that she was crying. He put his arm around her and told her, "Don't worry, the little cats will be safe and I will bring them home again, and we will have the video as proof."

She smiled at him. "You are so sweet, Alistair, I have really enjoyed these past few months, helping you and our little cats plan this adventure. It has been such fun."

They walked slowly back to their rooms, not speaking any more, just thinking of their intrepid cats and the big adventure they were about to go on. How excited they must be!

Alistair sat dozing in his armchair, dreaming of adventures he had experienced during his life time. He had been on many, but nothing quite like this one. He woke up when his tummy rumbled to remind him it was breakfast time. He stood up and walked to the dining room, giving a quick glance out of the window at the space shuttle, which was nicely shaded by the buildings, and hoped the little cats were okay. As soon as Alistair and Sarah finished their breakfast they were up and outside, taking a walk round all the rockets and spacecraft before ending up next to the space shuttle. Alistair gently tapped on the cockpit roof and heard Howard and Doris purring softly.

He whispered, "Are you both okay in there?"

A quick reply of, "Yes, thank you," came back. "We are quite excited now and cannot wait, this is fun," said Doris.

Howard said, "I missed my bacon."

To which Alistair replied, "Never mind, Howard, I will give you a whole slice when you get back."

They all laughed.

It was not long before the car park was full of people again. Alistair asked the cats to be quiet and said they would be back later to check they were still okay. Lots of people came over to talk to Alistair and Sarah and thanked them for organising such a wonderful event for the village of Lochcarron and surrounding areas. There were a lot of people here now who had not come yesterday, but had heard about it and decided to see the final stages of the Lochcarron space programme.

The head of staff came out and announced that refreshments would be available and everyone cheered.

Alistair said, "It is going to be another good day, I think."

As he turned to go inside a big transit van with aerials and a satellite dish on the roof, turned down Millbrae. He squinted to see what was written on the side, and was astounded to read, "BBC Scotland Outside Broadcasting Department."

'WOW!' he thought, 'It is going to be on television, who would have thought that?'

Chapter 20

A Television Crew Arrives

Alistair went back to his room and had just settled down in his comfy armchair when there was a knock at the door.

"Come in," he said and the door opened. A man and woman stood there with a camera and a microphone.

The lady came in and said, "We have been told that you are responsible for the events that have been going on this weekend, please could we interview you and cover today's events live?"

Alistair blushed. "I did have several helpers and I will ask my friend Sarah if she will take part, as I know the others want to stay anonymous. I do not mind as long as you give me time to wash and shave, I will meet you outside at 1400 hrs."

They all agreed and Alistair settled back in his chair to rest. He woke again about midday, had a good wash and a shave before putting on his best clothes.

He tapped on Sarah's door and a sweet voice said, "Come in."

She had been dozing on her bed and Alistair noticed she looked very tired and asked her if she was okay.

She sighed and smiled, "I was a bit tired after all the excitement and just needed to rest for a while."

Alistair sat beside her and told her that he was glad that she had been involved in the planning. After tonight, it would all be over and they could get back to their quiet life again. Before they could rest completely, though:

"We have the television cameras outside and they would like to interview us about the events over this weekend, will you help me?" he asked. "I have agreed to meet them at 1400 hrs, I need some rest as well, as it is going to be a late night."

Sarah smiled and said, "I will be by your side as I always was during the planning of the adventure."

Alistair thanked her and said, "I will come back and get you just before 1400 hrs, sleep well."

Alistair went back to his room and lay down on top of his bed and was soon fast asleep. His alarm clock started to buzz at 1345 hrs and he sat up and rubbed his sleepy eyes, and had a quick wash to smarten himself up for the television appearance. He made his way to Sarah's room just as she was closing her door. She looked up at him and gave a lovely smile. 'She looks very smart this afternoon,' he thought, and put his arm out to support her as they walked up the corridor to the foyer and out to the car park. A very smart couple, everyone thought. The television lady came over and asked them if they wanted to sit down, but both said they would be happy to stand or walk around the rockets.

She asked them, "How did you come up with the idea of the Lochcarron space programme?"

Alistair said, "We had watched some young friends looking at books on space travel, the moon and the stars and they got so excited about what was possible, so we came up with the idea together, but although our young friends did not want to appear on television, they are still a very important part of the programme."

75

Alistair went on to explain how the events had gone yesterday and that 10 would have been chosen to take part in the final launch tonight but due to an unfortunate accident in which an excellent entry had crashed and exploded on landing, only nine would be going tonight. Sarah then told the television lady that although this was the first Lochcarron space programme, she hoped tonight's amazing event would become an annual event. She explained that the final nine contestants would make their way to the top of the Bealach Na Ba, where at 2200 hrs the spaceships and rockets would have their second launch and this would be even more special now, as it would be captured live on television. The audience in the car park cheered as the cameraman panned around, zooming in on each of the entrants. As he zoomed in on the space shuttle, he suddenly stopped and looked again, he thought he had seen an eye looking at him, but he was obviously mistaken as it was not there now.

The rest of the afternoon passed quickly and after tea, everyone from the centre who was able were transported to the launch site, which was packed tight with contestants, television crew, spectators, fire service and mountain rescue and it was all very exciting. At 2200 hrs Sarah picked up the microphone and asked for quiet, a hush fell over the summit as she began to speak.

She thanked everyone for coming and all the contestants for their efforts. She told them that each rocket would be launched in order from nine down to one, the very impressive Lochcarron Garage space shuttle being last.

Each contestant launched as directed and shot their rocket into the air as the audience cheered and clapped. The cameraman videoed them as the television lady announced their names and bigger cheers echoed around the hills as they came back down. Out of eight that had launched so far, only one had a minor mishap coming back down, when it hit a rock and got badly dented, otherwise all was well with the Lochcarron space programme, live on television.

Chapter 21

The Launch Goes Ahead

As the No 1 space shuttle prepared to launch, Alistair made an excuse and went to sit in the minibus, from where he could see everything and still fly the shuttle as planned. He had carefully watched the man who flew it yesterday and knew that as the flame came pouring out of the back, it was time to launch. He watched even more closely as the man's hand moved and sent the space shuttle off into the sky. Alistair took control as the shuttle accelerated away towards Applecross; he made it bank to the right and gain height as it did so.

The poor contestant moved his controls, but to no effect, then shrugged his shoulders and placed his control box on the launch ramp.

He apologised and said, "I do not have control of it any more, something has gone wrong, I am sorry."

The audience watched in total amazement as the shuttle accelerated apparently on its own. Alistair looked at Sarah and winked as he pointed the shuttle towards the full moon that was sitting low over the mountains.

The shuttle got smaller and smaller in the distance and the audience started to disperse, saddened that the best craft on show had somehow failed on the most important flight and was now heading off into the distance, and it was anyone's guess as to what would happen to it. Alistair decided that he and the cats had had their fun and he would now bring the shuttle back. He pulled the lever back to slow it down and pushed another lever to the right so it would turn and head back towards them. He sat and waited but it never slowed, it never banked to the right. What was wrong? What about our lovely cats? What had he done?

Howard smiled at little Doris strapped in beside him. She smiled back and said, "This is fun."

Howard laughed and said, "I am now in control of the shuttle, because I knew that we would not get the full adventure we had planned with Alistair's radio controls, as it could only fly so far before having to turn back or crash. Our human friends have been very good but since the closing date, I have been busy reading books on flying and playing flight simulator games on the computer. I said this would be a great adventure and so it will be."

The Bealach Na Ba cleared slowly as the humans started to go home. Alistair and Sarah were now as upset as the men that built the shuttle, perhaps even more so as they were the only ones who knew the lovely cats were in it. What would the staff and the residents say when they noticed they were not about any more? The cameraman was still watching the shuttle going further and further away, it was still on a perfect flight path towards the moon and was even banking slightly to keep on the perfect course. He was a bit spooked now; a supposedly uncontrollable shuttle on a controlled flight path to the moon. How could this be? Then he remembered seeing the eye in the cockpit when he was videoing in the car park, but what could it have been? That is, if he had seen one at all. He would have to check the video later.

Chapter 22

There Could Be Trouble

Alistair and Sarah went back to their rooms, not speaking because they were so upset. Everyone was disappointed the space shuttle was lost, but only they knew Howard and Doris were strapped inside. Neither of them slept that night and they stayed in their rooms the next day. Staff brought their meals to them, but they could not eat very much as they were so upset that they could not do anything to help their two rather adventurous friends. They did not know that Howard and Doris were having the time of their lives.

After three days of not leaving their rooms and eating very little food, the staff called the doctor in. This was also about the same time the staff had spoken about not seeing Howard and Doris in their usual haunts, and the same day as the man from the television crew came back with his video of the shuttle sitting in the car park. This could be interesting, everyone thought, as Alistair and Sarah were brought along the corridor to the lounge. Both of them were asked to sit down and explain what was going on. The Lochcarron space programme had ended badly but it was not their fault, they had only organised it.

Alistair said, "You wouldn't understand."

The manageress asked them, "Have you seen your good friends Howard and Doris lately, as they seemed to have vanished into space, a bit like the shuttle really?"

This was too much for Sarah, who started to cry.

The cameraman spoke at this point and said "If you would all care to sit down and watch this video, it might go part way to explain some of what has happened."

So they sat down and looked at the screen.

The cameraman explained as they watched the video that when he was videoing in the car park, he was zooming in on all the spacecraft and when he first zoomed in on the shuttle he thought he saw an eye looking at him, but when he looked again it had gone, so he thought he was mistaken and had forgotten all about it. That night up on the Bealach Na Ba, he had seen Alistair leave the launch site and go and sit in the centre's minibus alone at the biggest moment of the night, the launch of the No 1 entrant, the space shuttle, but why?

"The launch was perfect and beautifully controlled," he said, "But then the owners and builders from the Lochcarron Garage said they no longer had control of it. But why was it still flying perfectly, if no one had control? This is when I saw Alistair, with another control box, sitting in the minibus, but what had happened after that?"

The cameraman said he had continued videoing as the shuttle headed on a perfect flight path banking to follow the moon, but at this point Alistair was heading home to the centre, so who or what was controlling it? The cameraman stopped the video as the eye showed through the cockpit window and you could just make out the little face of Doris. Everyone gasped and said, "How?"

The cameraman continued the video and highlighted the fact that they had been inspired by little friends who did not want to be interviewed, but would still be a very important part of the programme. Everybody looked at him as though he was crazy.

He said, "You have seen the video as well as listened to it, what other explanation is there?"

Alistair looked at Sarah, still crying beside him and shrugged. "Okay, I will tell you everything, but please don't be angry, we were just trying to help our friends, we did not mean any harm, honestly we didn't."

Alistair then told them the whole story from start to finish, well almost.

"A few weeks ago, we spotted Howard and Doris reading books and looking at things about rockets and space travel on the computer. We questioned them and they said they wanted to go into space, so we said we would help them."

Everyone looked at him as if he was mad as well, but he carried on, "They had two outsider friends; Pierre, a pine marten and Olivia, a short eared owl, who were delivering the posters to get people to build a spacecraft or rocket for them."

No one could quite believe what they were hearing. Alistair stopped for a minute and patted Sarah on the shoulder.

He said, "It's okay, it is for the best that they know," and continued his explanation, when there was a knock at the door and a young boy came in and asked Alistair if he could come with him. Alistair asked the staff if it was okay and promised he would come straight back and they all agreed. A break was a good idea anyway.

Chapter 23

Not How You Thought

Alistair followed the young boy to the parking bay at the side of the library and there, strapped on the back of a trailer, was the Lochcarron space shuttle.

"How? Where? When? What happened?" asked Alistair.

The young boy said, "I was coming back from Dingwall with my dad, when I saw something flying over the bothy in the glen as you come over the mountains from Achnasheen. My dad stopped the car as this flew up the road in front of us and just stopped, so we pushed it on the trailer and here it is, we knew you would want to see it."

Alistair asked the boy to run inside and get all the others and a screwdriver.

"You will be quicker than me," he said.

All the staff, the doctor, Sarah and the cameraman appeared around the corner and gaped in amazement at what they saw, the return of the Lochcarron space shuttle. The young boy gave Alistair the screwdriver and he got busy taking the cockpit canopy off, just as he had done previously and two little heads popped up and purred with excitement. They were home and safe after their big adventure. The staff took the cats inside and the doctor and the cameraman shook their heads in total disbelief. Alistair released the video camera from the rear of the shuttle cockpit and the young boy and his dad followed everyone back to the centre.

"This is going to take some explaining," said the manageress.

The doctor laughed and said, "Alistair I was very concerned for your state of mind but some of it seems to be true, let us see your video now."

They all settled down to watch Howard and Doris on their big adventure, and what Alistair said was apparently true, though it seemed far-fetched at the time. It was proven when Howard took control of the shuttle. Everyone smiled at the two heroic cats, two little Lochcarron cats, who had flown into space and managed to return safely. News of the return of the space shuttle soon spread around the area, but no one believed that Howard and Doris had organised everything until the mobile cinema came to the shinty field in July and everyone could see Howard and Doris's Lochcarron space programme and actual television footage from the car park and the Bealach Na Ba, plus Alistair's video from the flight. Lochcarron and district were proud of Howard and Doris, who promised to behave from now on, but not everyone believed them - least of all Alistair, Sarah, Pierre and Olivia - but they were all so pleased to have their two friends home safe again.

The adventures of Howard and Doris became an international hit both on television and the internet. Many visitors came to Lochcarron and the surrounding area to see Howard and Doris, view the Lochcarron Garage space shuttle and admire the stunning scenery that inspired the two little cats from the Howard Doris Centre to embark on an amazing adventure. Howard and Doris now had an adventure of their own to talk about, everybody that came to the centre always asked them for their stories now instead of them always listening to others. They would spend hours, if given the chance, to tell of where their adventures had taken them and all the exciting things they had seen. They never did make it to the moon in this adventure, but they had flown high up into the sky and not many cats can say that, can they?

Places that Howard and Doris visited on their world tour. How many can you find on a map?

Lochcarron

Catbrook (Wales)

Catford (England)

Catrijp (Holland)

Catz (France)

Katzenelnbogen (Germany)

Catalina Bay (South Africa)

Catak (Indonesia)

Cataby (Western Australia)

Catanga (Queensland Australia)

Kati Kati (New Zealand)

Cat Spring (Texas USA)

Lochcarron